SECRETS OF A SAGACIOUS WITCH

SECRETS OF A SAGACIOUS WITCH

A THAUMORIAN LEGENDS NOVELLA

A M ENO

First edition, 2024

ISBN
979-8-9893390-3-7 (ebook)
979-8-9893390-2-0 (paperback)

DEAR READERS AND REVIEWERS
A NOTE FROM THE AUTHOR

In my previous novella, Origins of a Guild Master, I wrote a promise to readers and reviewers to never respond to, share, or vilify negative reviews of my work. In the process of finalizing Secrets of a Sagacious Witch for publication, I debated removing this author's note as a way to avoid redundancies.

However, once again, readers who give any published work (indie or traditional) ratings under three stars are being attacked.

As an author, I have sympathy for these authors. I understand what it's like to put your heart and soul into a piece of work and have people dislike it.

My sympathy ends there, though. As a notoriously picky reader, I have had negative things to say about even the most flawless pieces of work. Vice versa, some of my favorite books of all time are extremely flawed in ways I simply refuse to acknowledge in the wake of my love for them.

All of this to say - my work is, and always will be, a safe space for readers and reviewers to share their honest thoughts. Whether they love or hate my work, finish, or DNF, I promise never to respond to, share, or vilify any reviewers leaving negative thoughts regarding my work.

Once again, thank you to everyone who has given my work a chance, and I hope you enjoy the adventure you are about to embark on!

Sincerely,

ALSO BY A.M. ENO

THAUMORIAN LEGENDS

Novellas

Released

Origins of a Guild Master

To Be Released

Dawn of a Ruinous Love

Creation of a Fated Thief

Heart of an Outcast Mistress

Novels

To Be Released

The Death Bringer

To anyone who has sacrificed everything, expecting nothing in return.

CHAPTER 1

Alopecia

Abdominal Aortic Aneurysm

Aminotransferase Enzymes

Acanthamoeba Keratitis

Jade listed diseases and physical ailments in her head.

Of course, that didn't include the magic-class-specific ailments. Such as dimiskid, a common injury where a Kinetic accidentally moved their kidney, caused by having a knack for moving people rather than objects. Or sedheo miskeria: a shifter-specific injury that occurred when they adjusted the size of their heart, making it too large for their chest cavity.

Achalasia

Achondroplasia

Acne Rosacea

Actinic Keratosis

Jade took a deep breath in and out.

Steadying herself, she approached the intimidating entrance to the Witch's University.

The memory of her first visit to the University crawled to the forefront of her mind. When her father stood with her before those looming doors and explained to a tiny Jade that attending the University took a lifetime of hard work and was the most selfless thing a Witch could do. A Witch had to dedicate every second to gain admittance, sacrificing leisure time, friends, and hobbies. And once they did, they would spend the rest of their life devoted to the service of others, the most noble thing a Witch could do.

Not long after, she fixed her first butterfly wing, pride blooming in her chest like a springtime flower. Shortly thereafter, her parents started taking her on regular trips to the surrounding jungles, teaching her how to use the other half of her magic, sensing how one flower would heal while another might induce death. All culminated in her final admission examination, where, with unflinching scrutiny, the Council had watched as Jade created a complex tea regimen with ingredients she had never heard of, seen, or touched before.

Everything had led to her first steps into the famed university, the most challenging institution in all of Thaumoria to gain acceptance. Its unmatched reputation produced the most esteemed healers.

And they had accepted her.

Actinic Purpura

The thud of her shoes echoed as she passed through the doors.

Adenoiditis

The building's lobby expanded around her. Grand and overbearing, with its domed ceiling, marble floors, and columns so large she couldn't wrap her arms around them.

And that was it.

A long, heavy sigh released the tension in her

chest. She was in. No one was coming to throw her out.

Glancing around the lobby, she took in the intricate paintings and decorations that adorned the polished stone walls and carved ceiling panels. Ultimately, she decided the whole thing was quite anti-climactic. Shouldn't her first moments among the esteemed ranks of University Witches be monumental?

Was that all she'd receive on the first day? She'd been working for over twenty-five years, a quarter of a century, to gain the right to walk through those doors. And all she got was a pretty view?

Jade wasn't sure what she expected. She just thought it would be... magnificent. A major introduction. An impressive initiation.

Jade reeled at herself, admonishing her attitude. It was a significant achievement, and she was doing what she always did: criticizing.

Her mother's words came to mind, making her sigh. *Not everyone can live up to your impossible standards. Not even you.*

She was doing it again, demanding that everything and everyone live up to or surpass her unreasonable expectations. Her hands wrung around the strap of her satchel hanging across her chest, determined not to spoil it for herself.

Looking around again, Jade was intent on taking in the grandeur. On second inspection, the art was beautiful—all the scenes depicted significant stories in Witch Mythology.

The time when the first Witches gathered, working together to cure their sister with magic. Radhera, Amethea, and Valedra would become the first healers. Their sister, Morrana, would be the first patient. All Witch beliefs were built around the four of them.

Then, there was the story of how the jungles surrounding the city came to be. Brought forth by the Four Sisters after they ascended beyond the living, teeming with plant and animal species that couldn't be found anywhere else in Thaumoria. Grown as a gift to a community who came together to save the Four Sisters' descendant, a nephew who would become a skilled apothecary.

A lineage of community was the Witch legacy. Nothing was more important than sacrificing yourself for another. Children belonged to all, and every Witch was her family. That's why healers were the most esteemed and sought-after profession among Witches. Nothing was as selfless as dedicating oneself to the service of others.

Jade continued through the lobby, turning down a side hallway and making her way to the lecture hall that would be her home away from home for the next several years. Already, two of her year-mates sat in the hall. There were about a dozen seats, but her class would only occupy half of those. And her class was one of the bigger ones.

With the university being infamously picky about who they admitted each year, the largest class in history only had ten students, the smallest being a class of one.

Choosing a seat near the front, she retrieved two notebooks from her satchel. One well-loved one containing her most significant notes and thoughts throughout the years written in her cryptic shorthand, a common practice among university students. The other was fresh and clean, the cover unstained, the pages un-ripped.

The rest of her class trickled in, taking seats scattered around the hall. A couple of whispered conversations started from those who had previously attended school together, but everyone was too tense to do much else.

The university strictly guarded the curriculum, expressly forbidding past or present students or teachers from discussing specifics of what they taught within those halls. None of the students knew what to expect going forward, but all were eager to learn.

A door opened at the back of the room, and sharp, staccato footsteps echoed through the hall as heels struck the hard floor. An imposing figure glided down the center aisle; her chin held high, hard, narrow eyes trained forward. It was like witnessing one of the Four Sisters themselves glide by.

Jade stared at the professor with reverence. Had there been more people in the room, she was sure there would have been whispers of admiration, but no one wanted to be *that* person.

Vitter, the most famed university professor and one of the four who made up the city council, formed as a part of the City Establishment Treaty to represent Witches as a people.

Everything about her was sharp and perfect. Not a single dark hair dared to fall out of place. Her cheekbones and jaw were sharp enough to slice through flesh and cut away a person's imperfections. Dark, narrow eyes scanned the six Witches sitting before her, analyzing everything about them.

The room was silent for several drawn-out moments. All the students held their breath, hoping they passed the exam none of them had prepared for.

"Congratulations," Vitter said, her hands moving as sharply as she spoke, signing in time with her words—a habit of any who grew up in the City of Witches to accommodate those hard of hearing. "Every one of you worked incredibly hard to sit in these seats. However, this is not the time to become lazy. Just because you have earned admittance does not automatically entitle you to graduation. This will be difficult, and some of you will not last until the end.

"Your education starts now. Welcome to the

university." Each clipped syllable ground against the students like a pestle, grinding them into a pulp at the base of a mortar. Professor Vitter met each of their eyes before turning to the board behind her and starting her lecture.

Looking around, Jade noticed three of her classmates had already started to sweat, ready to crumple under the pressure, including a girl just two seats down from her. The rest furiously flipped their clean notebooks open, ready to jot down everything Professor Vitter said. They all had their own treasured journal laid open on their desks, ready at all times.

Jade flipped open her new notebook to the first clean page and jotted furiously, writing a perfectly organized bullet-point list of everything the professor said. The lecture was long and exhausting. Professor Vitter covered the future of their education in detail, including every detail of etiquette the university expected them to follow.

From that day onward, the university expected them to dress the part of fully graduated Witches, including the uniform they would receive following the lecture.

They should consider any direction from a Council member as an order, and they were to follow it without question. Failing to comply would result in their expulsion.

There would be no explicit testing. Every moment they were within the university's walls was a test, and the students had to regard it as such.

All assignments would comprise true, real-time cases. Under the advisement of professors, the students would participate in diagnosing and healing of actual patients. There would be no more lectures from now on, no more formal classes.

By the end of the lecture, each student looked exactly how Jade felt—exhausted but enthralled. They were ready to take their first steps into the real world of healing. No more case examples from books. No more essays as long as their textbooks.

Jade was ready to begin the rest of her life.

CHAPTER 2

THE NEXT DAY, the class of six stood together in matching uniforms. Their professor had instructed them to wait for their first assignments in the lobby, and they each fidgeted in their own way, eager to start.

Fingers tapped. Toes bounced. Hands ran through hair. Jade wrung the strap of her satchel into a sweaty coil between her hands, the way she would twist a moist towel she would give to a patient.

But none of them spoke.

After an excruciating length of time, a short, graying man approached.

"Hello. My name is Professor Coshot. Follow me." He turned and promptly started further into the university, heading in the opposite direction of the lecture hall, not bothering to glance back to make sure they were following.

For a moment, the students all hesitated, exchanging confused looks. Professor Vitter had been quite clear the day before that they would work separately on their assignments. But their mentor for the day was walking away with no signs of slowing, so they scurried to catch up.

"Um… professor?" one student asked, voice shaking in time with his hands as he found the nerve to question orders.

Jade didn't recognize him, but that was to be expected as she was the only one from her preparation program to be accepted. The other students came from one of the other four programs throughout the city.

"Yes?" Professor Coshot didn't look back at the young man speaking to him, but his fist bobbed toward the student in acknowledgement.

The student looked back at the rest of them,

trying to find support. "We thought… I mean, yesterday Vitter told us—"

"Professor," Professor Coshot snapped. He repeated the movement of the word, his fingers practically spitting the correction. "It's *Professor* Vitter."

The student swallowed hard. He kept his signing small and close as he spoke, as though he were shrinking as the conversation continued. "Yes, of course. My apologies. Yesterday, *Professor* Vitter clarified we would work separately on our assignments."

Professor Coshot came to a jarring stop, causing the rest of the students to almost crash into each other. They had been walking in a tight formation to overhear anything the professor said and were steps away from a mortifying domino effect.

The professor's face showed no outright expression as he examined the young man before him, but his gestures oozed with irritation. Each flick of his fingers was terse and pointed. He clearly didn't appreciate being questioned.

"Things change, Mr. Helebor. Witchcraft is an

ever-changing practice. Adapt or leave. The choice is yours."

Helebor paled, looking more like a sickly patient than the healer, but Professor Coshot didn't give him a second glance. He turned and continued on his way. The rest of them followed close behind, but Helebor stayed back, away from the professor.

After several turns, Jade realized where the professor was heading. She'd volunteered there several times while building her University application. He was leading them to the patient wing, the only section of the university open to the public. People traveled from all over Thaumoria to seek help within those stone walls.

Soon, the students gathered before a window, a flock of curious birds eager to spot the first seeds of spring, peaking into one of the patient rooms. Professor Coshot stood in front of them, turning his back on the room to meet the eyes of each one of the students.

"Within this room is your first patient. Your assignment is to diagnose them. The patient is a fifteen-year-old Shifter who has been experiencing extreme chronic pain with no apparent cause. Questions?"

Jade was the first to speak up, her hands moving as fast as the wheels in her mind. "How long have they been experiencing the pain?"

"The extreme chronic pain started with puberty, at twelve."

Professor Coshot's wording caught Jade's attention, but another student spoke up before she could question further.

"What is their Shifting focus?"

"Facial structure."

"Theirs or others?"

"Theirs."

Jade took advantage of the pause to ask her next question as they contemplated the information. "The extreme chronic pain started at twelve. Were there any prior symptoms?"

The professor eyed her with care, analyzing her the way she would study a test question. Once again, his expression stayed neutral, but approval twinkled in his eye. "Yes. It came and went before twelve. Now, it is constant. Varying from tolerable to excruciating."

Jade tilted her head in thought. "Triggers?"

"None apparent."

That threw Jade off. Her instincts told her magic was the cause. It generally reacted to emotions, which became unpredictable and hard to control upon puberty. But with nothing triggering an emotional response, it ruled out most known ongoing ailments caused by magic. Which meant something natural was probably causing it, but that didn't feel right.

The other students continued their questioning, but Jade only partially listened. Taking in the answers without really paying attention, she ran through the symptoms of every known diagnosis that could be related, categorizing them by likeliness, from the unquestionably unrelated to those with the greatest chances of being correct.

Finally, they were all handed identical files, filled with every bit of information documented by all previous Witches who saw the Shifter. From their first appointment shortly after birth in the City of Shifters to their most recent visit with the unit's on-shift Witches.

Jade would look over the wealth of information once she was alone. At the moment, she wanted nothing more than to get into the room and let her magic do its thing.

The rustle of paper accompanied the constant buzz of the healing ward as her classmates started flipping through the file. Rather than follow in their stead, Jade approached the glass.

The room on the other side was a standard patient room, including the bed containing the young Shifter. They constantly moved, unable to find a comfortable sleeping position. Without end, their toes curled and flexed. Their legs repositioned without pause. Then, without warning, their entire body caved in as if trying to escape a phantom assailant.

Jade noted the dark hollows under their eyes, creased and squeezed shut, their entire face twisting with pain.

Beside the bed was a chair occupied by an older Shifter, a stone passing between his hands. Absently, he stared at the stone as his finger worked along the surface, pushing and pulling it, adjusting the shape with each pass. The equally dark circles under his eyes indicated he was the father. She double-checked the file just to be sure. Assuming wrong would be the epitome of embarrassment. Indeed, the father accompanied the young Shifter while their mother stayed behind in the City of Shifters with their two younger siblings.

"How do they sleep?" Jade asked, without realizing she had spoken.

"With aid," Professor Coshot quipped.

Jade glanced over her shoulder to find Professor Coshot studying her. "How often? And how much aid?"

"This is all in the file," Professor Coshot stated coldly as if already annoyed with having to babysit the students, though he continued to analyze her. There was a pause, where he expected her to flip through the file. But when she turned her attention back to the Shifter, he said, "Every other night. As much as is safe."

Jade's hand instinctively went to her throat, trying to calm the empathy rising in her chest. They were only getting sleep every second night because they were being pumped full of sleeping aides. That's a life no one should endure, let alone someone so young.

The young Shifter was uncomfortably thin, creating hollows in their cheeks where sallow skin stretched taught. It was a stark difference compared to their father's medium brown complexion. Even their partially shaven red-brown hair sat limp and dry where they had left it long on one side.

"May I?" Jade asked the professor without looking away.

There was a long pause. Long enough that Jade wondered if he was going to answer at all. And then he replied, "Yes."

Jade quietly entered the room, shutting the door with a slight click. On the patient's side of the glass, the air was heavy, weighing on Jade's shoulders like a winter blanket. The burden of the father's attention landed on her, drawn away from the smooth stone in his hand, scrutinizing every inch of her to ensure she was worthy of treating his child.

Jade approached him, using her free hand to

sign a formal greeting before holding it out to shake. "Hello, my name is Jade Sadore."

He shook her hand limply before dropping his gaze to the file she held to her side. "You're a new one."

Jade pressed her lips together. "Yes. I'm a student at the university. They assigned my class to your case."

A sad chuckle came from the bed, where the young Shifter, Tommie, sat up a little straighter. "Student, huh? Have they officially given up on me?" The words were callous, but their beautifully sad hazel eyes were warm if shadowed by agony.

The implication that she was lesser just because she was a student stung, but Jade understood where it came from and pushed the hurt down. "No. A Witch would never give up on someone in need. The university believes you would benefit from more minds working together."

"Sure. I've heard that one before."

Tommie groaned, squirming on the bed as a wave of pain struck. Tommie's father, Bron, stuck the stone in a pocket and walked to his child's side, rubbing their back as the suffering crested. Jade imagined it was the only thing making Bron feel useful while watching his child writhe. The helplessness written across Bron's face was so clear she read it like a textbook.

"As I'm sure you know, this isn't the first place we came. Many Witches have promised to help, and they all told us they couldn't do anything." Bron sighed, an undertone of anger leaking through his words.

Jade bowed her head, unsure of where to go from there. She tried to remember everything she'd learned about bedside manners. About comforting the hopeless, those who very well may have every right to be hopeless. Having written several essays on the matter, she consistently earned top grades for her understanding of patient psychology.

But crafting the perfect reply was so much easier when the patient was merely a written question on paper, responding however she imagined they would. Even more so when Jade could rewrite the answer a dozen times, taking days to find the right words.

Looking into the eyes of a jaded young Shifter who couldn't sleep or sit still because of the unexplainable was so much different. A young Shifter who had no reason to hope for peace.

She searched for the right words, but none of the pre-planned ones she'd devised seemed acceptable at that moment. Instead, once the wave passed and Tommie and Bron relaxed, she went with the only thing she could think of.

"I'm sorry. What you're experiencing isn't fair, and you have every right to feel as though others have given up on you. But I promise, we're here to help. Or at least… try."

Bron dropped back into his chair, exhaustion pulling at the bags under his eyes as he ran a hand over his face.

Tommie sat back against their pillows with a long, heavy breath. They watched Jade without really looking at her, as if remembering a time of normalcy they'd never experienced. They stared through her for so long that, for a moment, Jade thought they wouldn't answer.

But then their hand fell to the mattress, stretching out against the rumpled sheets.

"Then try."

Jade made her way to the chair next to the bed, seeing the last glimmer of hope shine in Tommie's eyes. Perching on the edge of the chair, she took a deep breath and placed her hand in theirs, palms meeting.

Her magic jumped at the chance to be used, immediately flowing through the Shifter's fingers, connecting them. Jade probed with her magic, letting it slide along the Shifter's bones and muscles, exploring their veins. She worked her way deeper until her magic wrapped around Tommie's heart. Their heartbeat drummed, and Jade experienced the powerful rhythm as if it were her own.

With every new inch Jade's magic explored, firing nerves assaulted her. Constant pain signals went off, making it hard to focus on anything else. Jade tried to figure out why the nerves were firing, but everything presented as normal on the surface. No broken or fractured bones, no organs out of place or malfunctioning, and no skewed blood vessel ratios. She pushed harder, trying to find…. something. But aside from the over-reactive nerves, she couldn't find anything wrong.

Jade bit her lip. An idea came to mind only because she'd always been told she *shouldn't* do it. You never, ever, *ever* mess with a person's nervous system without extensive training. The nervous system was such a unique specialization that very few Witches even sensed the nerves, let alone affected them. Doing so incorrectly could affect a person forever.

Jade retreated, pulling her magic back. When their hands released, Tommie studied Jade's face, a sad attempt at a smile pulling at their lips—an attempt at hope.

"Well?"

Jade shook her head, trying to catch her breath. "It's… it's hard to get past…"

"The pain. I know. That's what they all say." Tommie sighed, resigned to the reality of their life. Their face shifted ever so slightly, the corner of their eyes turning down, making their sorrow even more prominent.

"I'm sorry," was all Jade could think to say.

Tommie smiled weakly. "It's not your fault."

Jade clenched her fingers in her lap to keep them from shaking with the aftershock. Standing, she turned to leave, suddenly feeling useless.

"Will you come back?"

She spun to find Bron watching her, the stone jagged where it rested between his fingers, the barest shimmer of hope in his bloodshot eyes.

"Excuse me?"

"You said Witches never give up," Tommie said, grimacing as their ever-moving legs squirmed beneath the sheets. "But we've seen plenty of Witches once and never again. Will you come back?"

Jade swallowed hard, unmerited determination straightening her back as she glanced from Tommie to their father and back. "Of course. I'll be here every day if need be. I've never left a puzzle unsolved."

Bron snorted, attention returning to the stone, lost in thought.

Tommie's mouth twitched at the corners in something close to amusement. "Ya know, I'd believe that."

Jade stepped out of the room as her class-mates entered one by one. Moving to the side, out of sight, she fell back against the wall. The air was significantly lighter outside the room, inflating her lungs effortlessly.

Professor Coshot waited nearby, coolly watching her every movement. "Find an answer?" Despite the lack of intonation to the question, something about it felt sarcastic. As though he already knew the answer.

Jade squeezed her eyes tight, pushing away the memory of agony clawing at her chest. Shaking her head, she opened the file in her hand, ready to dive head-first into the problem. "Not yet, but I will."

CHAPTER 3

"You should have seen the look the Sage gave us when they found us climbing out of the fountain." Tommie beamed, white teeth gleaming in the light of the setting sun. Today, their eyes were round and upturned, cheekbones soft, giving them an innocent look that showed just how young they were.

They waved their hands, talking animatedly as they told the story of the time they had been playing tag with their siblings in the Shifter Temple, and all three of them fell into the lobby fountain.

Jade laughed, covering her eyes with a hand.

The second-hand embarrassment turned her cheeks red. For the first time in days, the room's atmosphere was light and playful, laughter floating through the air like mist after a light rain.

"What happened?"

Tommie shook their head, giggling. "Our parents signed us up for Temple duty for a month. We spent half the summer cleaning prayer rooms and greeting patrons."

Jade chuckled along with them, unable to keep from joining in their rare glee. "You're lucky the Sage is so understanding. I can't imagine how the Witches Council would have reacted to something like that."

"Not so tolerant?"

Jade sighed. "Let's just say a month would have been absolutely nothing."

Bron entered the room, handing Jade and Tommie each a glass of water.

"Thank you." She sipped the cool water before setting the glass on a nearby table. "Tommie was telling me about their summer cleaning prayer rooms."

Bron snorted, taking his usual seat in the chair

in the corner. He stretched his legs, leaning back to get comfortable and pulling out a new stone. "Which time?"

Jade's mouth fell open. "What?"

Tommie blushed, cheeks becoming rounder and more childlike, sinking lower into their stacked pillows. "It's a really easy fountain to fall into."

"It is. Especially when you push your brother over the edge, and he pulls you in with him."

Jade burst out laughing again, and the other two followed with their own fits of chuckles. Joy bubbled through the room, popping when a cry of distress pierced them.

Tommie doubled over, arms wrapped around their middle as they groaned. Jade placed a hand on Tommie's back, trying to soothe them by simply being present. Bron sat forward in his chair, steepling his hands before his mouth as though he were praying.

That became their pattern over the previous three weeks. Each afternoon, Jade would head to Tommie's room, and they would start with a check-in. How were they feeling today? How was the pain? How often were the episodes occurring? The answers were always the same, but the spasms were clearly becoming more frequent by the day.

During the first week, she often crossed paths with one of her classmates, doing their best to find the answer they were all searching for. But by the second week, she saw less and less of them. By the third, she hadn't seen them once. Neither Tommie nor their father mentioned whether the other students were coming by, and she hadn't asked. She didn't want to know the answer.

Jade only controlled how often she came by, and that was what was important.

Over the days, grimaces turned to tears as Tommie clenched their teeth to hold back a cry. The duration of intense, overwhelming, all-consuming torment increased from seconds to minutes, each one more heartbreaking than the last.

Each time, Jade would move to the bedside, placing a hand on Tommie's back to let them know they weren't alone. She attempted to use her magic more than once during one of the episodes. Each time, she thought she got a little closer to the answer, and each time, the onslaught of firing nerves would become too much. Her magic would only last a few heartbeats before she had to pull it back to save her sanity.

Easing pain was easy, one of the most rudimentary of skills among Witches. But to do it, she had to understand what was causing it. Otherwise, her efforts were useless. Her magic couldn't ease what it couldn't find. If it had been an isolated break in the bone, only the nerves in that particular area would fire, which would have been easy to navigate. But they were firing across Tommie's entire body.

If she was going to figure out what was happening beneath the pain, she had to understand how to push past it. How to see through it.

She would need to practice. How, was the question?

The episode ended, and Tommie took a deep breath, falling back against their pillows.

Bron sighed. "You doing ok, kiddo?"

"Fantastic," Tommie breathed, closing their eyes. All their features seemed to flatten, becoming neutral and indiscernible as their shoulders drooped.

"How about I talk to the Witches on staff and have them administer your sleep aides?" Jade offered, eyeing Bron.

He gave a slight nod. She hoped he would also sleep, but he wouldn't leave that chair. The same way he hadn't since the two of them arrived. He ate in that chair, napped in that chair, and worried in that chair.

Tommie didn't answer. Instead, silent tears slipped down their cheeks as their fingers clenched and unclenched, staring off at something that wasn't there.

Jade stepped out of the suddenly tense room, closing the door quietly behind her.

Glancing through the window, she saw Tommie's lips tremble, caving as sobs overtook them. The sobs shook their entire body. An echo of despair leaked through the windowpane, barely audible through the glass. Bron went to the bed, pulling his child close and holding them as they wept. Pressing a cheek to their hair, he silently cried with them, sharing in their grief for the normal life they had never gotten to experience.

Not wanting to intrude on an intimate moment, Jade turned away. No matter how hard it was to witness, she had no right to join in their grief. She shifted her focus, instead, to the circular desk buzzing with activity in the middle of the ward.

"Can you please administer Tommie's sleeping aid in about fifteen minutes?" Catching the attention of someone on duty, she hoped that would allow enough time for the intimate moment to pass.

"Miss Sadore, you're still here."

Turning, Jade found Professor Coshot signing off on a document on the other side of the Witch's station. He didn't say it like a question, but she nodded anyway.

"Yes. I've made it a point to visit the patient every day."

Professor Coshot didn't look up from the documents he flipped through. "Yes, so I've heard." He handed the file off, his hard eyes scanning Jade. "Why don't we take a walk, shall we?"

Again, it wasn't so much a question as a command. As a student, he expected her to follow all orders without question. They fell instep beside each other, not saying a word until they reached the small galley down the hall.

"Have you made any progress on the Shifter case?" Professor Coshot didn't bother to ease into the conversation. He got straight to the point, gaze penetrating, hand movements blunt.

Jade took a deep breath, suppressing a sigh. "No."

"I see." Professor Coshot filled two glasses with large chunks of ice and water, handing her one. Jade suddenly remembered her mostly full glass sitting in Tommie's room. The proper thing to do would be to go back and get it, but she couldn't bring herself to walk back in there.

Professor Coshot sipped his water, watching her closely. She couldn't tell what he was looking for, but she hoped she passed whatever test it was.

After a tense moment, Professor Coshot started away from the galley before stopping and turning to face her again. "Might I offer you some advice?"

Did she have a choice? "Of course."

"Understand your scope of magic and understand when it is ineffective in a given situation."

Professor Coshot didn't wait for her response. He walked away without another glance over his shoulder.

Jade stood there, speechless. Was he telling her to give up? To walk away and admit defeat before she'd done absolutely everything in her power to help someone?

Indignation surged through her, turning the edges of her vision red. Her fingers tightened around the ice-cold glass in her hand, knuckles turning white. The taste of blood flooded her mouth as her teeth bit into the side of her cheek to keep her tongue in check.

How dare he suggest she couldn't solve it, that she might fail out of the university before ever having time to succeed? And what about her classmates? Was he suggesting she was the least competent in her year? That her magic was somehow *inferior* to theirs?

If Professor Coshot was suggesting she

request a different case, then he was out of his mind and didn't know a single thing about her.

Jade gulped down a mouthful of the frigid water to help calm the blazing fire within her, screaming to be vindicated. Distracted by her anger, a large chunk of ice slipped past her lips, pressing against the roof of her mouth.

The sudden shock of piercing pain went straight to her brain. The ice rattled against her teeth as she tried to move it away from the sensitive flesh, but that only made it worse. Squeezing her eyes shut, she fought against the sudden stab and spit the ice cube back into the glass. Doubling over, the pain peaked. Her brain seemed to push itself through her eye socket, and she had to press the heel of her palm against it to hold it in.

Taking deep breaths, the pain faded as quickly as it had started.

Jade swore under her breath, fighting the urge to throw the glass. With each day, her exasperation grew, turning into outright anger. Anger at herself for being an inferior Witch. Anger at Professor Coshot for suggesting she walk away from someone in need. And anger at her classmates for not caring enough to show up and comfort a disheartened patient.

But as the last stabs faded away, Jade got an idea.

ICE CLATTERED against the sides of a metal tub in the center of her small bathroom as she dumped out the last sack. Her apartment (if one could even call it that), provided by the university, was barely large enough to hold the single bed, dresser, desk, and bookcase that had been there on her arrival. The adjoining bathroom was even smaller. Barely enough space for her to turn around in. Maneuvering the metal tub into a usable position had been a trick all on its own, but she'd managed.

It took a significant amount of convincing before the kitchen staff handed over the loads of ice. The bags of ice were already melting by the time she lugged them back to her room. It would be worth it, though, if it worked.

She just had to push past the pain.

Systematically, she stripped off her shirt and trousers, leaving her underclothes, sightlessly watching the sloshing ice water as she did.

Working mechanically and focusing on her breathing, she didn't give herself time to think about what she was doing.

Before she talked herself out of it, her hands gripped the edges of the metal tub, and she plunged one foot into the icy water.

Gasping, she instinctually yanked her foot out of the piercing cold. Clenching her teeth so hard she feared they might crack, she stopped her escaping toes. Slowly, she forced her foot back beneath the frigid surface.

Every inch was a challenge. It took every cell and bit of focus in her stubborn body to force herself into the tub, and when the cold hit her chest, just the act of breathing became agonizing. Sucking in one ragged breath after another, she fought to keep from crying out.

Ignoring the need to scream and cry was difficult, but she forced them down. She didn't want anyone to hear how insane she was if it didn't work.

Tears rimmed her eyes, but she refused to let them fall. Her entire body shook, refusing to accept the circumstances she was in. Clearly, Jade was going into shock, and if she didn't control herself soon, her body would force itself out of the tub. If she gave in, she would have to repeat the process all over again.

Fingers clenching the edges of the tub, knuckles turning white, she turned all her focus to her breathing. One long breath through her nose. Then another. Closing her eyes, she pushed her magic inward. Every inch of her body in contact with the ice burned, her nerve endings screaming that something was wrong. Warning bells rang through her body, overwhelming her senses and her magic.

The experience was exactly the same as when she used her magic on Tommie.

Jade took another steadying breath, focusing on delving deeper than the pain. Pushing past it until she discerned what lay beneath. Silencing the noise and forcing it into the background.

As Jade cleared her mind, her magic found her heartbeat and held steady. She counted the way she would when taking vitals on a patient. When she took a full count (ignoring the alarming rate at which it raced), she let her magic work on instinct. It slid along her bones, slowly going deeper until it inspected her organs. The feeling was comforting. One she'd experienced hundreds of times. Completing her examination routine, she grasped the familiar, pulling it close.

Blood pressure.

Blood oxygen.

Not temperature. She didn't need to know that right now.

Jade checked every inch of her skeleton, knowing full well there were no broken bones. She double-checked that each of her major organs were functioning correctly. And soon, she found the noise of her pain dulled. It wasn't any less *there*, but she'd been able to dampen the noise, like listening to a cheering crowd from behind a thick pane of glass.

At the exact moment she realized it, she lost it. The control slipped through her fingers, dissolving into the surrounding water so fast it almost hadn't existed at all.

Jade jumped up, gasping as a stab of cold assaulted her once again. She scrambled out of the freezing water so fast she tripped on the tub wall. Jade cloaked her shivering body with the towel she had laid out beforehand, trembling so badly that she would have been concerned if she had been one of her patients. But she only smiled, sucking down gulps of air.

Pulling her knees to her chest, she leaned against the bathroom wall and laughed hysterically.

CHAPTER 4

THE CHAIR next to Tommie's bed creaked as Jade settled into it. Her fingernails dug into her palms as she fought to keep from fidgeting.

"How are you feeling today?" she asked, starting their meeting the same way she always did.

Tommie shrugged, closing the book they'd been reading. "Oh, same as usual. I'm practically dancing through the halls." They smiled weakly before doubling over, moaning.

Jade grabbed their hand and rubbed their back. When Tommie started to wretch, Jade grabbed a small pail and held it to their chest.

Tommie's meager lunch became reacquainted with the light of day, as it often did.

They grew thinner with each day, unable to hold down hardly any food due to the gut-wrenching episodes.

Bron held his head in his hands, elbows resting on his knees. The tears floating in his hollow eyes weren't visible behind his palms, but they had become an ever-present glisten. Tommie wasn't the only one growing thinner by the day.

When the spasm passed, and their stomach was once again empty, Jade cleaned up and returned to their side.

"I don't think I can do this anymore," Tommie whispered, wiping the tears streaming down their cheeks.

Jade took their hand in hers, holding it tight. "You can't give up. Not now."

"Why not? We haven't gotten any closer to a diagnosis, let alone treatment or a cure. I'm living on sleeping aids. What kind of life is this?" Their eyes were glassy, the tears emphasizing their hazel swirls.

Jade shook her head. "Let's try again. Maybe this time will be different."

Over the last week, Jade had repeated the ice baths twice daily, once in the morning and once more before she went to sleep. Each time, her ability to push past the pain came quicker and stayed longer. When she eased herself into the frigid water without losing control of her body and performed her entire internal examination without getting distracted, she knew she was ready to try again.

She hadn't told Tommie or Bron about her experiments with the ice bath to avoid getting their hopes up, but she was betting everything on them.

Tommie hesitated, then nodded their consent.

Jade closed her eyes, taking several deep breaths, preparing herself for the onslaught of sensations.

Slowly, cautiously, she pushed her magic, sliding along Tommie's veins and easing her way beneath the skin. The ever-firing nerves struck her immediately, pummeling her with an uproar of pain signals.

Jade let her magic still without pulling it back. Focusing, she pushed the noise to the back of her mind as she had in her ice baths. The process was far more taxing when it was on someone else and took every scrap of her attention. But after several tense moments, she started her routine, breathing deep and letting the noise fade.

Without the constant uproar overwhelming her, she gradually pushed deeper, letting her magic ease further along Tommie's bones. Jade performed her normal internal examination, and once again, everything came back normal, but she wouldn't admit defeat yet. Her magic sat still, eased by the normal functioning of Tommie's body as the seconds ticked by until another spasm started.

Half a second before Tommie doubled over, the slightest shift sent a domino effect through their body. The spasm threw Jade out of Tommie's body and back into her own as it hit in full.

She fell back in her chair, gasping for breath, trying to find herself again. Spending more than a few moments with her magic deep within another was always disorienting. The longer she spent, the harder it was to come to terms with herself again.

Jade didn't give herself time to adjust. Now that she understood, she could help. As Tommie cried out, tears spilling onto their sheets, Jade grabbed their hand again, sending her magic in without hesitation.

Rather than diagnose, she eased.

Her magic worked to counteract the firing nerves, encouraging them to settle. Working to convince Tommie's body that everything was normal. Since she understood, she sent out reverse signals to dull the agony.

With more time and understanding, she could counteract it all together, but this was completely new territory, and the pain was everywhere. It spread her magic too thin.

As her magic fought to normalize things, Tommie breathed easier.

"It's… it's working," Tommie gasped. A mixture of confusion and relief faded into a form of relief in their hazel eyes. "You're doing it. It's working!"

Bron's head snapped up, eyes wide as he whipped his gaze from Tommie to Jade.

Jade trembled, her magic depleting quicker than she anticipated. But Tommie held a hand to their mouth, tears of joy flowing freely. For the first time, their legs stilled, their fingers stopped clenching, and their shoulders relaxed.

"Please, dear Aais…" Bron whispered behind his interlocking fingers.

Tommie sobbed loud, body-shaking sobs that echoed through the room—a sob of relief.

After a minute, they gasped hard, their entire body going rigid again. Their legs resumed squirming, but they weren't as frantic as before.

Tommie turned to Jade and pulled her into a hug. "It worked! You did it."

Bron rose from his chair and kneeled beside the bed. "I can't believe it." He held the hope in his voice back from fully blooming.

Tommie hugged their father, nodding vigorously.

Jade reveled in her pride only for a heartbeat before shoving the feeling down. "But only for a moment. It's already back, isn't it?"

Tommie smiled, wide and beaming. "It doesn't matter. It worked. I experienced a few seconds of peace for the first time in years. It was the best feeling in the world. How did you do it?"

Jade shrugged, not wanting to celebrate too soon. She didn't quite understand what she'd experienced or found. She didn't know how to fix anything. But she could provide bits of relief, and for the moment, that would have to be enough.

"I just pushed past the pain."

Tommie shook their head in disbelief, still smiling as their fingers clenched and unclenched around Jade's hand.

"So what is it?" Bron asked. "What's causing this?"

Jade swallowed hard, trying to remember everything she'd learned about breaking hard news, but she recalled none of it.

"It's… their magic. Their bones are Shifting."

Tommie and Bron exchanged identical looks of confusion, brows gathering, a silent conversation passing between them.

Tommie stared down at their squirming legs, trying to understand. "But… that doesn't make any sense. My Shifting focuses on facial structure." Their high androgynous cheekbones softened as if to prove a point, eyes widening as their orbital bones changed slightly. Small shifts that made them appear more feminine. "I can do that without it hurting, so why does it hurt everywhere else? Why can't I control it?"

Jade thought back to all her classes on magic-specific ailments. Mentally flipping through her notes and textbooks, she scanned the pages until something struck her.

"Before I continue, understand that I am only theorizing what is happening. This is not an official diagnosis. For that, I must first meet with my advisors and have them confirm my suspicions."

Both Tommie and Bron nodded. Jade shifted uncomfortably, not wanting to give them any wrong information.

"Shifters who can shift their and others' appearance often have far more complex magic than they realize. The ability comes so naturally that they focus on the outcome rather than the process. What we've learned, though, is when a Shifter affects things like facial structure, they're not just targeting the skull. They're also affecting the skin, nerves, muscles, veins, etc. By doing this, they negate any painful side effects of the shift.

"When magic operates outside its designated focus, it doesn't always work the same way. What I think is happening is that your magic is striking out in response to outbursts triggered by the constant distress the magic causes. It targets your bones without muting the nerve endings as it normally would."

Tommie stared off to the side, eyes unfocused, taking in the information. "So… my magic is pissing itself off?"

Jade shrugged a single shoulder. "I suppose you could describe it that way."

"So why hasn't anyone noticed it before?" Bron asked.

"I suspect they haven't been able to push past the overwhelming sensation of constant nerve signals. The bone shifts are small and almost imperceptible, even without the overwhelming pain, but the nerves never stop firing because they're constantly growing and shrinking. Small shifts cause the constant aches, whereas bigger shifts, triggered by the never-ending pain, eventually causes the episodes. The difference is minuscule in theory, but the results are very intense."

Tommie let their head fall against the pillow, pressing a palm to their forehead. "I can't believe it. You actually did it…"

Bron clapped, bouncing where he kneeled as if infused with renewed energy. "So what now? What do we do? How do we fix it?"

Jade smiled. "First, I need to run everything past my professors. I assume they will want to confirm my findings. Once they do, we can immediately start looking for a treatment and possibly a cure." Jade's heart swelled with pride.

"What are you waiting for, then?" Tommie beamed. "Run!"

Jade smiled back, squeezing Tommie's hand one last time before starting toward the door.

"Jade, wait!"

She turned as Bron made his way over to her. "Yes?"

Tears of joy and relief streamed down his face, staining the collar of his worn-out shirt. "Thank you," he whispered. "Thank you for not giving up."

Jade couldn't think of anything to say, so instead, she smiled back briefly before taking off, darting out of the room and down the hall.

———

A DULL SYMPHONY of voices leached through the thick, plain, wooden door with a single plaque in the middle that read: *Office of Professor Vitter.*

Alopecia

Abdominal Aortic Aneurysm

Aminotransferase Enzymes

Swallowing hard, she smoothed out the few stray hairs that freed themselves from her tight black bun. After asking nearly a dozen people throughout the university, someone informed her that Professor Coshot was meeting with Professor Vitter and that she could most likely find him in her office.

All Jade had to do was work up the courage to knock on the door.

Interrupting an important meeting for

anything less than the most necessary circumstances would automatically target her for quick
dismissal from the university. But it *was* the most
necessary of circumstances, wasn't it?

Her fist hovered over the door.

Acanthamoeba Keratitis

Achalasia

Achondroplasia

Before she could talk herself out of it, she
rapped her knuckles against the wood—three
sharp taps infused with urgency.

She retreated a step, waiting for the door to
open. The voices inside stopped before the door
opened a crack, revealing Professor Vitter's severe
features.

"Yes, Miss Sadore?" No kindness warmed her
eyes, though her words were cordial, a clear
warning in her penetrating glare. It had better be
important.

Jade squared her shoulders. "I have something
very important to discuss with Professor Coshot
regarding the assigned Shifter's case."

Professor Vitter's dark, hooded eyes narrowed
ever so slightly. "I'm sure whatever you need to

discuss can wait until he is available." Professor Vitter made to close the door, but Jade stopped it with her hand before thinking through the action.

Appalled by her brazen gesture, Jade yanked her hand back. "Please, professor. This is urgent."

Professor Vitter's eyes darkened as they considered her. The silence stretched on for an eternity, but Jade didn't back down. She needed to be heard.

After a moment of consideration, Professor Vitter opened the door the rest of the way, stepping back so Jade could enter.

The small office had just enough space for the desk that split the room down the center, an oversized cushioned chair on one side, and two decorative chairs on the other. Professor Coshot occupied one of those decorative chairs, while a Kinetic man Jade didn't recognize sat in the other.

He was about her age, sitting back in the chair casually, one foot crossed over a knee. He wore a gray suit with perfectly shined shoes, and his gray-green eyes scrutinized her.

"Miss Sadore, how can we help you?" The

smallest waver in Professor Coshot's tone showed how surprised he was by her presence.

Jade's gaze darted between the unknown man and the professor, carefully selecting her words so as not to stutter. "I'm sorry to interrupt, but I need to talk to you about the Shifter case I've been working on."

The Kinetic's analyzing gaze held a knowing glint, clear as he hung on every word.

"We are in the middle of something. Can't this wait?" Hardness edged Professor Coshot's words, his unchanging expression shadowing.

"That is okay. I think a break is in order, anyway." The Kinetic man stood, straightening his suit without taking his gray-green eyes off her. "How about we pick up this meeting tomorrow, shall we?"

Professor Vitter cut Jade a fierce glare before turning a softer expression on the Kinetic.

"Of course. We will see you then."

The Kinetic stopped on his way to the door, holding his hand to Jade. "It was nice to meet you. Miss Sadore, was it?"

She took his hand out of politeness if nothing

else. She needed him to leave immediately. "Yes. Nice to meet you too, Mister…"

"Please, call me Malachi." A small, polite smile pulled at his lips before he exited the office, closing the door behind him with a click.

"Miss Sadore, what in the name of the Four Sisters could possibly be so important?" Professor Vitter spat through clenched teeth.

"I did it," Jade rushed, nearly cutting off the end of Professor Vitter's question. "I know what's wrong with Tommie."

Silence blanketed the office, weighing on her shoulders until they threatened to slump under the pressure.

Jade hadn't expected heaps of praise or verbose flattery for her achievement, but she expected… something. Instead, the professors stared at her, unmoving, unshakeable, before looking at each other.

Jade had to keep herself from biting her lip. The silence stretched on and on, the tension in the room growing by the second, until finally, Professor Vitter met her gaze again.

"Explain." Her hands gestured slowly,

drawing out the request with guarded movements.

Jade took a deep breath, smoothing her hair again. Glancing between Professor Coshot and Professor Vitter, she hoped to find something other than skepticism, and failed.

"The reason no one has found a diagnosis is that the sensation of the nerves firing has been too much. It's been drowning out our Witch magic." She spoke slowly and signed clearly, each movement crisp and precise. If she rushed through her explanation, she would seem frantic and lose the respect she so desperately needed.

Professor Vitter sank into her chair, her back stiff as a board, taking care with every movement she made. "And we are to understand this was not a problem for you?"

Jade shook her head. "No, it was a problem, but I found a way to push past it. By doing so, I discovered the cause of the pain."

Professor Vitter didn't answer. Her narrow, hooded eyes pierced Jade to the core, making her heart race. Everything about the woman was fierce. From her sharp cheekbones to her perfect black hair smoothed back into a tightly twisted bun, she was the epitome of unflappable. Even her clothing was crease and wrinkle free. Professor Vitter was everything Jade had aspired to be since she first learned about the university as a child.

And she was looking at Jade with an expression that could cut through steel.

When it was clear Professor Vitter would not continue her inquiry, Professor Coshot picked up where she left off. "What do you believe to be the cause?"

Jade pressed her lips together, shifting her focus from Professor Vitter to Professor Coshot, but the weight of Vitter's attention never left her.

"It's their magic. Tommie's bones are shifting by micro-amounts. The shifts trigger the nerve endings, and their constant state of agitation eventually builds into a spasm. The shifts are so small they are difficult to detect beneath everything."

Difficult, but not impossible, she wanted to add, but it was the wrong thing to say at that moment.

Professor Coshot dipped his head in acknowledgment, like he needed the time to take in what she was saying, before looking at Professor Vitter again.

"Well," Professor Vitter started, her hands flipping open with an exaggerated flourish, that single word like a slice from a blade. "I suppose we should go confirm your findings."

Jade nearly sagged with relief, but one last look at Professor Vitter's piercing stare told her it wasn't the time to relax. If anything, she became even more rigid as the three of them exited the office.

CHAPTER 5

TOMMIE'S ROOM had never seemed as small as it did with Professor Coshot and Professor Vitter standing next to the bed across from where Jade sat in her usual chair.

Tommie straightened in their bed, giving Jade an encouraging smile, while Bron swayed in the corner. He was uneasy about having so many people surrounding his child, but he didn't want to interrupt anything that might put an end to their suffering.

Sweat prickled at the base of Jade's skull, threatening to stain the collar of her shirt, but she smiled anyway. She didn't want Tommie to know how much pressure that moment held, but it would have been impossible for them not to notice the tension thickening the air.

Jade swallowed. "So, Tommie, with your permission, what will happen is that Professor Vitter, Professor Coshot, and I will all use our magic at once. Theirs will be present to observe and confirm my suspicions, while I will repeat our session from earlier. Do you understand?"

Tommie nodded, head bouncing with enthusiasm despite their ever-twisting legs and fingers. They held their hands to the side, offering themselves up for the experiment. "Absolutely. Anything you need."

Jade tried to smile, but the effort was meek, and her lips quivered.

"Thank you. This shouldn't take long," Professor Vitter assured them, her gaze far warmer than Jade had ever seen it. When her eyes flicked back to Jade's, though, they were once again coated with icy scrutiny.

The professors each placed a single hand on Tommie's arm, preparing for Jade to show them what she'd found.

Taking Tommie's hand in hers, she closed her eyes in concentration. For it to work, she had to block out the strain filling the room. Screwing up would mean no second chances.

She took one deep breath, then another, and then let her magic do its thing. Slowly, but more sure of herself, it pushed beneath the surface. Since she knew what she was looking for, the minute shifts were apparent along the edges of her mind, so small she would never have noticed it otherwise.

Carefully, she dulled the pain, working against the sensation from the shifting bones. Slowly but surely, she worked her way deeper, cautiously making each move. She was like a young Witch navigating the jungles on their first foraging trip, concentrating on every placement of their foot so as not to step on anything harvestable.

Seconds stretched into minutes, which stretched into an eternity. Jade couldn't tell how slow or fast time moved, concentrating on nothing but easing.

Soon, Tommie stilled. Their legs calmed beneath the sheets, their fingers relaxing. They let out a relieved sigh, letting their head fall against the pillows, soaking in the normalcy.

As the pain cleared, the shifting of Tommie's bones became easier to detect, but only minutely. For someone to find it without knowing what they were looking for would take an extraordinary amount of concentration.

Thankfully, the professors did.

Jade pulled back before her magic depleted, satisfied that she'd given the professors enough time to confirm her findings.

Confidence welled in her chest.

She'd done it. She solved the unsolvable puzzle. There was no denying it.

Grinning, she looked up, ready to see a sheen of pride in her professors' eyes, only to slip when met with nothing but a deathly glare.

Professor Vitter wore a mask of calm, refusing to let her emotions surface, but her eyes told a different story. Jade had never seen such anger and wanted to wilt beneath that stare.

What had she done wrong?

The professors removed their hands, and

Professor Coshot let a soft smile grace his lips as he turned to address Tommie.

"Thank you for allowing us this opportunity. Please excuse us; we will need a moment to step out and discuss things with Miss Sadore."

The way Professor Coshot turned and walked out without ever making eye contact horrified Jade. Professor Vitter followed, but not without giving Bron a small nod of assurance.

When the door clicked behind them, Jade was supposed to follow, but she couldn't bring herself to stand.

"What's wrong? What happened?" Panic laced Tommie's whispered words.

Acidic dread burned the back of Jade's throat. She didn't know what she would face when she walked out that door, but the chances of it being praise for all her hard work were minimal. Shaking her head, she forced herself to her feet.

"I don't know." Her voice trembled as she spoke, unable to find the comforting tone she'd practiced for so many years. She tried to meet Tommie's panicked expression but turned away the moment tears stung the back of her eyes.

Instead, she stared at their hands, their fingers still wrapped around hers. "I'll be back as soon as I can." It was meant to be reassuring, but the way Tommie squeezed her fingers let her know it wasn't.

In the hall, she found the professors whispering between themselves, silencing the moment she approached.

Professor Coshot passed her, heading back to Tommie's room. As he did, he patted Jade on the shoulder. A gesture of comfort so out of character it did nothing but make her knees buckle.

"Follow me," Professor Vitter snapped. She turned on a heel, taking hurried but controlled steps down the hall and away from the ward without bothering to check that Jade followed.

They turned into the first empty room they found. Professor Vitter ushered Jade inside before closing the door behind them.

"Miss Sadore, explain yourself." Professor Vitter commanded in a low, barely controlled voice, barely finishing one sign before starting another.

Jade opened her mouth to answer, her jaw

hanging open before snapping shut. No words came.

"I don't know what you were trying to prove by that stunt, but I assure you it will never happen again."

"Stunt?" Jade had done the unthinkable. She did exactly what they assigned her to do. She exceeded every expectation. What about her last exhaustive weeks had been a stunt?

The professor continued as if Jade hadn't spoken at all. "Exploiting the desperation of a child and their father in the hopes of obtaining, what? Glory? Did you think we would simply take your word on what you claimed to find?"

"Of course not!" Jade cried, horrified by the accusation.

"Then what did you think this performance would accomplish?"

"Professor, it wasn't a performance! I found the diagnosis. I did as Professor Coshot asked of me. You must have felt it!"

"Neither Professor Coshot nor I experienced anything of the sort. What we did observe is an untrained student toying with the nervous system of a patient who is already in severe distress."

Jade froze.

They didn't feel it... all that time, all that work, and they didn't feel it. Every moment since she had stepped foot into the university blurred, blending into itself until she was sure it had all been a dream. It was impossible; it couldn't be happening. She'd done everything right, and yet, she was under scrutiny because they didn't feel it.

"Taking advantage of a family in their time of need, endangering a patient by manipulating the nervous system without training, shall I go on? If this was an attempt to pull ahead in your class, I can assure you that—"

Jade cut off the Professor's ranting. "What did the other students find?"

"Excuse me?" she seethed.

"The other students," Jade repeated, choosing her signs carefully. "If they didn't come to the same conclusion I did, what did they find?"

"They did what was appropriate and stepped away when they realized the case was out of their scope of expertise."

"B-but the assignment—" Jade stuttered.

"The assignment, Miss Sadore, was to understand when you are unfit and step away when necessary. Students were not supposed to find a diagnosis. We assigned you an unsolvable case on purpose. The first lesson every university student must learn is how to fail."

Students were not supposed to find a diagnosis… Jade repeated the words in her head but couldn't understand them. No matter how she broke it down, she couldn't fathom how those words came together in a sentence.

Students were not supposed to find a diagnosis…

"But… but the expectation…" Jude muttered, stumbling over the words whirling around in her head.

"Some expectations aren't meant to be achieved," Professor Vitter spat.

Jade heard the words come out of Professor Vitter's mouth. Understood them on an individual basis. But the meaning of them spoken in verse together was lost on her. It was like the professor was speaking an entirely different language.

Jade couldn't fathom how someone could string those syllables into a phrase like that. There had never been a time in her life when she hadn't met the expectations laid out for her. Every standard her teachers set, every grade her parents asked her to make, and every assignment her former teachers and professors had tasked her with were all meant to be completed and exceeded. She couldn't understand a world where someone would punish her for doing what they asked of her. Where they asked her to do something without being expected to actually do it.

And what about Tommie… their father… was she supposed to walk away and leave them to suffer? If they expected Jade to remove herself from the case, and the professors couldn't feel the bones shifting, who would find a treatment? Who would work on a cure? Was everyone going to sit back and watch Tommie die a slow, excruciating death as their body shut down from lack of food and sleep?

Jade was at the Witch's University. It was supposed to be a place of innovation and healing. Where those in need went to be cured. To be heard and cared for. No case too big, no case too small. No case too complex or complicated.

Witches don't give up on patients.

The entire foundation of Jade's world crumbled beneath her feet, giving way to a spiral of doubt.

"Miss Sadore," Professor Vitter snapped, drawing Jade out of her plummeting thoughts. "I seriously suggest you think long and hard about your future here at the university and never, under *any* circumstances, pull a charade like that again."

Professor Vitter turned and left the room, slamming the door behind her, leaving Jade alone in the dark to think about her life choices.

CHAPTER 6

THE SWEET SCENT of florals and freshly turned earth floated around Jade as she sat on the floor of the university's greenhouse. Both her notebooks laid before her on the stone flooring.

After Professor Vitter left her to ponder everything she'd ever known, Jade walked mechanically to the greenhouse. That was where she had intended to go after the professors confirmed her diagnosis and cleared her to work on the treatment. It hadn't occurred to her to change that plan.

Tucked away in a back corner, she stared at

her two notebooks. One pristine with a single bullet-point list written out on the first page, detailing Professor Vitter's lecture from the first day, followed by a handful of pages of scribbled notes on Tommie's case. The second was well-used, loved, and filled her life's work.

She'd expected some classes and traditional lectures with a gradually increasing amount of hands-on experience. Instead, her brand-new notebook, which her parents had bought just for her first year at the university, sat nearly blank. There were no classes, no lectures. In fact, she didn't feel like she'd learned anything.

"Hello?"

The sudden break in silence made Jade jump. Searching between bushes, a person stood on the other side, watching her. The Kinetic from Professor Vitter's office was peering at her from around a potted bush, straightening the sleeves of his gray suit.

"Oh, hello…"

Startled, Jade rushed to gather her things, closing her notebooks and holding them close to her chest. Black strands of hair fell into her face, having freed themselves from her bun as she scrambled to her knees. Embarrassment flushed her cheeks, burning her face until she knew they were bright red.

"I'm so sorry; I'll be out of your way in just a moment."

The man held out a hand. "No, no. Please, do not concern yourself with me. I just saw you here and wanted to ensure you were okay."

Jade sat back on her heels, staring at the ground before her and pushing the loose strands of her hair behind her ear. Making eye contact was impossible. Jade felt like she might melt right into the floor if she had to look into the face of a stranger who had just caught her wallowing in the corner like a child.

The Kinetic shoved his hands deep into his pockets, and a long, awkward silence passed between them.

"Are... you alright?" he asked, the words clumsy as if he wasn't used to comforting others but was trying his best.

Jade glared at the floor, thumb rubbing against the cover of her notebook. "I'm fine."

"Of course."

Jade's shoulders went rigid, feeling mocked, though she was sure that wasn't his intent. "Can I help you find something?" she snapped, looking for any excuse to take the focus off herself.

The man cleared his throat as if he abruptly recalled where he was. "No, but that would certainly make this less awkward."

Jade snorted, glancing up at him from beneath her lashes. She expected him to be watching her, but instead, he was studying a nearby flower she couldn't identify.

"Actually, I was wandering the grounds and recognized you from earlier in the professor's office. I wished to speak with you."

Never taking her eyes off him, Jade got to her feet, adjusting the strap of her satchel on her shoulder. "About?"

"You seemed quite insistent earlier. Determined to speak with Vitter. I was wondering what about?"

Shoulders falling, Jade sighed. "I had what I thought was a diagnosis regarding a patient."

His head tilted, thoughtful as he examined the pale flower. "Thought? Were you wrong?"

Jade's head snapped up, dark eyes narrowing. "No." She spat the word before she thought it through, suddenly not so sure it was the truth.

"Then might I ask what you are doing here… studying? Should you not be working to help the patient?" He made a vague gesture between where she'd been hiding and the notebooks clutched tightly in her arms.

Jade dropped her gaze. "They didn't believe me."

The weight of the Kinetic's gray-green eyes roved over her. Not lustfully, the way some men did without realizing it, but curiously. Like he was trying to solve a puzzle she held the answer to. If only he could fit the pieces together.

"Why not?"

Jade's nose scrunched incredulously. "I don't know."

"But… you are sure you are correct in your diagnosis?"

Mulling the question over in her mind, she nodded.

A thoughtful silence settled as the man plucked the flower he had been studying, letting it hover midair, spinning slowly so she could see each individual petal.

"Then what do you intend to do about it?"

Jade whipped her head up, taken aback by the audacity of the question. "Excuse me?"

Something glimmered in his eye as he studied her, like a child poking an insect to see if it would curl up in the dirt or fly away.

"Well, you intend to do something about it, no?"

He was goading her. She could tell with how his words lifted with amusement, poking and prodding without being cruel.

Jade couldn't help it; she took the bait, unable to stand someone questioning not only her abilities but her will to act. Especially a stranger. "What am I going to *do*? I'm one wrong step away from being expelled. There's nothing I can do."

"Can or will?"

Jade gaped at him. "And who exactly do you

think you are? Last time I checked, *you* aren't a professor here."

He chuckled, using a finger to spin the hovering flower that had become stagnant. "No, no, I am not. In fact, I am nobody important."

She doubted that if he was having private meetings with Professor Vitter, but she wasn't about to say that out loud. He stepped forward, his flower moving with him as he languidly shortened the space between them.

"I am simply someone who studies words, and I find your choice of them quite interesting. You seem like a competent young woman."

"I am," she bit.

He smiled at the floor, amused at her building irritation. "And yet," he continued as if she hadn't spoken. "You choose to say there is nothing you *can* do when I am certain the word you are looking for is *will*. You *can* find a treatment, correct?"

He stopped a mere foot from her, the flower hovering between them like a barrier. Tempted to reach out and pluck it from the air, Jade clutched her notebooks tighter, bending the covers as she seethed.

"Of course I *can*. They wouldn't have accepted me if I couldn't." How dare a man she didn't even know invade her moment of peace just to insult her intelligence?

The Kinetic plucked the flower out of the air like a wineglass, the petals filling his palm, what remained of the stem peaking between his fingers.

"How interesting." With that, he turned away as if he made to leave, just like that.

Enraged, Jade stepped into his path. "What exactly are you trying to imply?"

Despite Jade's best penetrating tone, the man continued to look amused, which only infuriated her more.

"I would never be so bold to imply anything. I simply find the hypocrisy of your decision fascinating."

He lifted a single shoulder in a casual shrug. His matter-of-fact movements grated against her, digging at her already crumbling self-esteem. She opened her mouth for a rebuttal, but he continued without bothering to wait for her reply.

"I have spent a significant amount of time studying Witch culture. If I am not mistaken, one of the first things a Witch learns is to trust their magic, correct?"

Jade clenched her jaw so hard she thought her teeth might crack but nodded nonetheless.

"Then, it is reasonable for an outsider, like myself, to see your decision not to help someone because another does not believe you as going against that important moral. No?"

Jade didn't answer. She didn't have the words. Agreeing with him would mean she truly wasn't doing everything she could as a Witch. Disagreeing would be an outright lie because he was right, and she instantly despised him for it.

"Any direction from a Council member is to be considered an order and is expected to be followed without question," she recited, repeating the rule, word-for-word, given to them on their first day. "Professor Vitter, a Council member, demanded I step away from the case."

He shrugged again as if that was nothing more than a mere inconvenience. Stepping into her space, he loomed over her. Not threateningly, but like he was about to whisper a dare in her ear. "If there is anything I have learned in my time, it is that some expectations are not meant to be achieved."

Jade heard the smile in those quiet words, thrown like a weapon that stuck her square in the chest. They froze her in place, gluing her feet to the stone floor.

Stepping around her, the Kinetic man left her there, stunned. The flower hovered where he had once stood before finding its way to her hand—the delicate petals, soft as velvet, pale against her flushed skin.

She might have stood in that spot for seconds, or minutes, or hours, watching the space he no longer occupied.

He couldn't possibly have suggested... no. That would be insanity. But she could... also, no. She might as well march herself right down to the City Guard and turn herself in for malpractice just for considering it.

But...

Jade had said it herself.

She *could* create a treatment.

She was a Witch, down to every speck of magic infused with the blood flowing through her veins, and she *could* create a treatment.

Pulling her lip between her teeth, she thumbed the petals, hesitantly probing at the flower with her magic.

Witches specialized in one of two types of magic: the body or the cure.

Witches who specialized in the body could do what Jade had been doing with Tommie. Send their magic into the body to sense what was wrong and fix issues of varying degrees, often with aid from elixirs, salves, oils, etc.

Others specialized in the cure. Those Witches often had the ability to sense the properties of plants and turn them into something more. They created things such as the pain medication and sleep aid Tommie had been using and the elixirs that aided those who specialized in the body. Together, there were few things Witches couldn't work together to treat.

Jade was capable of both, as was every student of the university. It was a requirement to apply, let alone be accepted.

The flower in her hand had pointed corn-silk petals that overlapped, spreading wide to expose three dark stamens jutting from the middle. Her magic intertwined with the properties of the flower, examining it the way she did the human body. Calling forth the properties, she sensed how it would affect the body.

Bones. The flower affected a person's bones, creating a stabilization effect. She got the feeling that if taken over time, it would strengthen them, reversing the effects of diseases such as osteoporosis when combined with the proper amplifiers.

Jade's stomach roiled with unease. She couldn't believe she was even considering the words of someone she couldn't remember the name of. Somehow, though, his words made more sense to her than anything else that had happened that day.

Tommie's bones were shifting; Jade was sure of that. Why the professors couldn't feel it didn't really matter if she knew for a fact she was right, right?

She shook her head, trying to clear it of her

traitorous thoughts. Of course it mattered! How could she even think differently? Not only were they some of the most powerful and experienced Witches in all of Thaumoria, but their magic was vastly more sensitive than hers.

Wasn't it?

Was it possible Jade truly felt something the professors couldn't? And if that was true, shouldn't they reward her instead of threatening her? Should Tommie be the one to bear the punishment for the professors' poor judgment?

And what about Tommie? Was their quality of life worth risking for Jade's continued position at the university? Didn't that go against everything Witches stood for?

The legacy of Witches, as established by the Four Sisters, was a lineage of community. Nothing was more important than sacrificing yourself for another.

Jade used to think sacrifice meant giving up her free time and social life for the sake of education. But what if it meant so much more? Would the Four Sisters smile upon her for listening to Professor Vitter, or would they scorn her for not giving up her future to help someone in need? Someone whose only chance was her?

Creating a treatment was her duty as a healer, her sister's responsibility as a Witch. Tommie's life wasn't worth sacrificing for her own. For her position in the community. She could do it. She could sacrifice everything to help a single patient.

And it would be *everything*.

By treating Tommie without the permission and oversight of the professors, she would be committing malpractice, and they would turn her over to the City Guard. They would lock her away for life to ensure she never endangered another person. Malpractice was the most serious offense among Witches, considered by the Council to be along the same line as flat-out murder.

And Jade was considering it.

She had to.

The only solution she could think of was to create the treatment and run. Stories of Witches who treated patients illegally all over Thaumoria circulated everyday. No one could prove it, of course, but no matter how hard the Council strived to extinguish the rumors, they still ran amuck.

Those of good standing frowned upon such Witches in the community, but they had to exist. Jade was going to bet her entire future on it.

CHAPTER 7

AFTER HOURS HUNCHED OVER A TABLE, flipping through her notebook filled with remedies, spells, and herbal combinations, the muscles of Jade's back were tied in knots. It had taken some creative thinking, and two of the most potent poukafe leaves she could find, but she had finally figured out the base treatment she would work from.

A combination of treatments for two different ailments should do the trick.

The first was einpath multiemotia. An Anima-specific affliction, which occurred when they became overly sensitive to all animals' emotions (as opposed to a specific specious or individual creature). It often led to an inability to distinguish their own emotions from an animal's, creating a snowball effect that eventually led to a mental breakdown.

The second would be sedheo miskeria, which occurred when a Shifter accidentally adjusted the size of their heart, making it too large for their chest cavity.

The treatment Jade intended to create would combine the emotional and magical regularity of the first with the counter effects and Shifter specialization of the latter. It should create an elixir that would mask the shifting of the bones, regulate their response to emotions, and make the magic more manageable.

It wasn't a cure, per se, but it would counteract the constant distress.

Sitting up straight, Jade stretched her sore muscles. The scratching of pencil on paper was the only sound as Jade made a list of all the ingredients she knew for a fact she would need. There were only a few she'd have to improvise, and one was sitting on the table beside her, practically glowing in the low light.

Every time she caught sight of the flower's face, she sensed that it was watching her, encouraging her to keep working. Delicately, she picked up the flower, spinning the stem between her thumb and forefinger.

For the hundredth time that night, she considered what she was doing.

What if she was wrong? What if she only *thought* the bones were shifting because she so desperately wanted to feel something? Then, everything she was doing would be for naught. If she was wrong, making it all up in her head, the treatment could do more harm than good.

But if that were the case, she wouldn't have been able to counteract the effects. It wouldn't have worked if she'd been wrong.

She hadn't manipulated the nervous system and how it fired; she had essentially masked the shifting of the bones to calm the nerve endings. Jade was right. The bones were shifting, and she *could* make a treatment.

Plucking a single petal, she thanked the flower

for its contribution. Using her thumb and fore-finger to crush the petal, oil coated her skin, and her magic focused once again on sensing the properties within the flower. She had to be sure of herself.

Vaguely, she wondered if the Kinetic chose the flower on purpose or if he selected the perfect one by mere coincidence. It was far too purposeful of a choice to be an accident, but there was no way he would've known about Tommie and the diagnosis Jade had come to.

Or had he?

Shaking her head, Jade decided that, ulti-mately, it didn't matter. The details of how she'd gotten there weren't important. All that mattered was that she was doing it and had made her choice.

Plucking another petal, she imbued it with magic, pulling forth the focus on bone health and pushing away the strengthening component. Placing it in a bowl, she ground the petals into a paste that would eventually separate so she could extract the purified oils. All the while, she quietly chanted in the old Witch's language.

The words of the Four Sisters.

———

JADE WALKED down the halls of the university, head held high. She clutched the strap of her satchel, wringing the material until her knuckles were white.

Deep within the satchel were two vials of the elixir she'd taken the entire night to create. Normally, she would have tested the elixir repeatedly, using small doses to ensure its safety and that it had the results she intended. Unfortunately, that wouldn't be an option.

She needed to be done quickly, in and out, before anyone noticed her presence.

Keeping her gaze steady, she watched only what was directly in front of her to avoid eye contact.

Soon enough, the door to Tommie's room came into view. Her heart pounded in an erratic rhythm, and she was sure one of the nearby Witches would hear the way it fought to escape her ribs. Each step seemed to echo through the halls, calling attention to her every movement.

All she had to do was get there, give them the elixirs, and return to her room. The whole thing should only take a few minutes, but those were minutes she couldn't afford.

She didn't acknowledge another person as she opened the door, slipped inside, and quickly shut it behind her.

"Jade?" Bron noticed her first, standing from his usual chair.

Saying nothing, she moved to the window, shutting the curtains.

Tommie sat up straighter in their bed. "What are you doing? They said you were being reassigned."

Jade hurried to the bedside, sitting in her usual chair.

"Say nothing. Both of you, I need you to listen." She kept her words quiet but rushed. No one could overhear their conversation.

Bron came to the bedside, and the three of them huddled together. "They told us your diagnosis was wrong."

Something pierced Jade's chest, but she pushed down the hurt. "I know, but they're wrong. Please, I need to do this quickly." She rummaged through her satchel, searching for the two vials.

Fear tinted Tommie's hazel eyes. "Why? What's going on?"

Jade pulled out the vials, pressed them to Tommie's palm, and covered their hand with her own.

"I know what they told you, but I trust my magic." She swallowed hard, looking deep into their hazel eyes, silently begging them to listen and believe. "Please, if you trust me, please listen."

Tommie nodded.

"Leave."

"But…" Bron started, but a quick glance from Jade silenced him.

"You won't find the help you need here. I made you a treatment. Leave and take it as soon as you step outside. Any sooner, and people will get suspicious."

"You…" Tommie's eyes went wide, staring

down at their palm, tears threatening to spill onto their cheeks. "You made a treatment," they whispered as if saying it themselves would make it real.

"Yes."

Bron pressed a hand to his mouth, closing his eyes in relief.

"Take one of these as soon as you leave. It should last until you get home. Take the other and find a Witch who specializes in cures. Find one who can replicate this sample without asking too many questions about where you got it."

That was it. That was all she needed to say. She'd done the impossible, and it was time to run.

Tears ran down Tommie's cheeks, leaving streaks along their tanned skin. They clutched the vials close to their chest, holding them against their heart.

"Thank you," they choked out.

Before Jade stood, Tommie pulled her into a crushing hug. Jade squeezed her eyes shut, wrapping her arms around Tommie for one quick embrace before pulling away.

Jade searched for words, for anything to say,

but came up empty. Instead, she said what she wished someone would say to her. "It's been my pleasure to work with you. You're going to do great things."

With that, Jade went for the door.

As her hand touched the handle, words came from behind her. "We won't tell anyone."

Jade paused but couldn't look at Bron as he spoke. It was too painful. If she turned, she'd have to face what she was doing. Acknowledge everything she was sacrificing.

"Your secret's safe with us."

Jade pressed her forehead to the cool wood of the door, letting her shoulders slump. She wanted to cry. To sob right there in that room. But walking out with tears on her face would give everything away. So, instead, she opened the door and walked away without looking back.

As Jade distanced herself from what she'd done, her breathing became easier, the stress coiled around her lungs loosening. She'd made her decision, and there was no going back. All she had to do was go back to her room, grab her things, and head for the train station.

"Miss Sadore, what are you doing here?"

Jade froze. Even her heart stopped beating for a long breath. Looking up, she came face to face with Professor Coshot.

She swallowed hard, trying to remember the excuse she concocted earlier and failing. Her tongue tripped over the words she tried to say, fingers unable to find the words.

Professor Coshot kept a stoic facade as always, his expression utterly unreadable as he observed her fumbled attempt at an excuse. When it became clear Jade couldn't give a coherent answer, he prickled, silencing her stumbling.

"I see." His eyes darted to Tommie's room behind her. "Are you satisfied with your choices today, Miss Sadore?"

Jade's eyes went wide as she clenched her jaw, nodding once.

Professor Coshot studied her for so long that she wondered if he would say anything. Finally, he gave one long, drawn-out nod.

"Then I suggest you continue on your way. Quickly." He stepped around her, heading for

Tommie's room, before looking over his shoulder at her. "It's been a pleasure."

The smallest smile played on Jade's lips, but she didn't have time to linger. With or without the professor's blessing, her actions were still against the law. Professor Coshot was giving her a head start, and Jade wouldn't waste it.

CHAPTER 8

STANDING IN THE TRAIN STATION, what little Jade owned hung off her shoulders, her satchel off one, her duffel bag off the other. Ignoring the people hurrying around her, she adjusted the weight of the bags.

She didn't like trains much, though if she were being honest, she had never actually been on one. The basic concept of how they ran made sense. Kinetic magic working in tandem with Fire Wielder magic seemed like a logical combination, yet they still made her uncomfortable. They were too big, too loud, and too fast. Just the thought of riding one had her clutching at the strap of her bag, but she didn't have a choice.

Of course, two significant problems stood between her and her safety.

The first was that she was borderline broke. University students didn't receive payment for their time. Instead, they had all their housing, food, and supplies paid for, as so few of them were accepted. Just enough coins sat in her pockets to pay for a single ticket. One way. So she better be sure of where she was going.

Which led her to her second problem: where to go. She had never been outside the City of Witches, except for her few foraging trips to the outskirts.

Jade understood the different magic classes. The way their magic worked and all the unique ways it manifested. She had to if she was going to treat them. But she had never considered *living* among any of them.

Of course, the cities all had diverse populations, but their main demographic always corresponded with their leadership. The City of

Anima was largely made up of Anima, but not entirely.

She shifted on her feet, looking over the schedule posted next to the ticket booth.

A familiar voice caught her attention. "Miss Sadore, it is nice to see you again."

Jade spun on a heel.

"It's you," she blurted, so on edge she couldn't control the words falling from her mouth so fast her hands barely caught up to them.

The Kinetic man nodded, tucking a book beneath his arm and adjusting the sleeves of his gray suit like a nervous habit. "Indeed, it is. Might I ask… what are you doing?"

Jade was tempted to stammer out a nonsensical excuse for being at the train station so he wouldn't run back to Professor Vitter and report where she was going. But Jade didn't know where she was going, and she was certain he wouldn't tell a soul. He was the one who'd told her to do it, after all.

"I'm… leaving." Saying the words aloud turned them into a palpable thing, wrapping around her heart and constricting it until it hurt.

He gave a pointed nod to the duffel bag hanging off her shoulder, lips lifting ever so slightly at the corners. "Yes, I see this. But why?"

He was going to make her say it. Make her admit what she'd done.

Jade searched for the words, but admitting to leaving had been hard enough. Admitting the truth of what she'd done… that would take time. Instead, she stared at the stones beneath her feet in shame. She should have been proud of her actions, and in time, she would be, but at that moment… she couldn't bring herself to confess her sins out loud.

Somehow, he understood the words hidden beneath her silence.

"I see." He nodded, pressing his lips together as if to suppress a knowing smile.

Jade sucked on her teeth. "Please, say nothing until I'm gone. I have no right to ask such a thing, but please—"

He took a step closer, cutting off her rambling. "Miss Sadore, did the professors ever tell you why I was at the university yesterday?"

She shook her head.

"I have come to the City of Witches, more specifically to the university, in search of a… business partner of sorts."

Jade's brows creased in confusion. "I don't understand."

He had encouraged her to break the law, go against the professors, and sacrifice everything… because he wanted to work with her? Not only did that seem like a cruel test, but an illogical one. Wouldn't he want to work with someone who was good at following orders? Who would want a business partner who couldn't conform to rules?

"I guess I am inquiring as to whether you have decided on a destination."

She shook her head, watching him closely out of the corner of her eye.

"Might I make a suggestion, then?" He stepped forward again, holding out a hand with a single silver coin glittering in his palm.

Hesitantly, she took it, running her thumb over the crest stamped on it—the symbol of Elementals.

When she looked back up, the Kinetic was already walking away, disappearing into the crowd. She raced to catch up, clutching the coin in a tight fist.

Twisting and turning, she ignored the pointed looks thrown her way as her bags crashed into people.

Catching up, she stopped him with a hand on his arm. He paused, looking down at her as though he didn't know what to do when someone touched him.

"Yes?"

She pulled back, squaring her shoulders, trying to find some of the confidence she had just weeks before.

"I'm sorry. I don't remember your name."

His lips gave the smallest of quirks. "You may call me Malachi."

That moment between them in the crowded train station felt important, like a shift in not only her own life but among Thaumoria as a whole. Once again, he was asking her to make a choice. Go to the City of Elementals and join his mysterious business, or disappear into another city, left to her own devices to learn the way of the world outside of the Witches.

Making up her mind, Jade stuck out her hand. "It's nice to meet you, Malachi."

Something in his gaze softened as he took her hand, giving it one firm shake. "It has been nice meeting you as well. I look forward to working with you."

With that, he turned again, slipping between patrons and disappearing from sight.

Jade looked at the coin in her hand once again, exploring the topography of the ridges beneath her fingers.

City of Elementals it would be, then.

ACKNOWLEDGMENTS

As my second novella, Secrets of a Sagacious Witch has supplied its own unique struggles during the publishing process. Most notably, the desire and need to live up to the expectations put in place by Origins of a Guild Master. Throughout the process, there have been several people who have been the wall against which I lean, holding me up and supporting my dreams.

First and foremost, my husband Joel, who has held my hand every day of this process. He reminds me why I write, as well as encourages me to walk away when I need a break. He is my Maquin, my Ove, and my Ian (and is one of the only people in the world who will understand what that means).

To my beta readers, who have become a team on which I draw my strength. I am the absolute worst at communicating with anyone who isn't within arms reach, and while they are no different, they continue to read whatever I send their way. They have cemented themselves as my first loyal readers, and I regularly find myself rereading their encouraging words to remind myself why my anxious thoughts are wrong.

To my cover designers at JV Arts, who truly outdid themselves with this cover. They took my obscure descriptions of "an old university (think Ivy League schools such as Harvard, Oxford, etc), with touches of purple" and truly brought the story to life. Book covers are an author's first way of marketing their work, and this one truly captures the essence of this story.

To my editor, Sydney Rain, who has become just as excited about this series as I have. Who, ever so kindly and sweetly, terrifies me with each new revision she sends my way. No matter how difficult it is to read, I know her critiques are for the best, shaping my work into what I imagine it is when I send it to her.

To my family, who has devoured the first novella and are biting at the bit for the second. I never expected this level of support from them, and it has been overwhelming in the best way. I truly thought Origins of a Guild Master would come and go, fly under the radar, and be forgotten as my first piece of work, and they have truly made it feel like the most important thing ever to be published.

Last but not least, I am grateful for every person who has taken a chance on a random author they found online and then proceeded to make it this far. Everything I write would be for naught if it weren't for readers like you. Whether you are a first-time reader or a newly dedicated fan, I am thankful for your time.

Forever grateful,
A.M. Eno

ABOUT THE AUTHOR

Originally from Howell, Michigan, A.M. Eno travels full-time with her husband and two cats. In 2017, she earned her Bachelor of Science from Black Hills State University, majoring in Psychology and a minor in Sociology. As a life-long avid reader, she hopes to create worlds and characters that invite readers to fall in love and feel at home. She strives to write high fantasy series that are a safe space for people of all backgrounds.

Printed in the USA
CPSIA information can be obtained
at www.ICGtesting.com
JSHW072248040224
56591JS00009B/27

9 798989 339020